We're Going on a Bear Hunt

STICKER ACTIVITY BOOK

Michael
Rosen

This book
was filled in by:

....

....

Helen
Oxenbury

WALKER BOOKS
AND SUBSIDIARIES
LONDON · BOSTON · SYDNEY · AUCKLAND

D1421873

We're going on a bear hunt!

Help the family find the bear by drawing
a path through the maze.

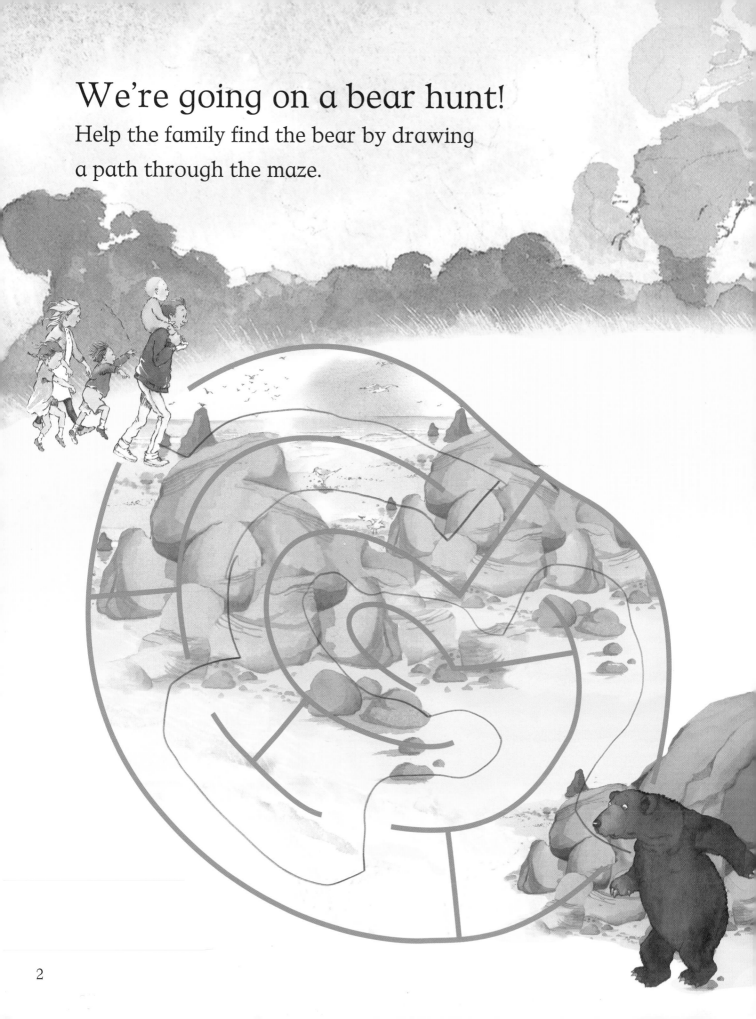

Picture sudoku

Find the stickers to complete the grid:
each row and each column should have
one bear, one girl and one boy.

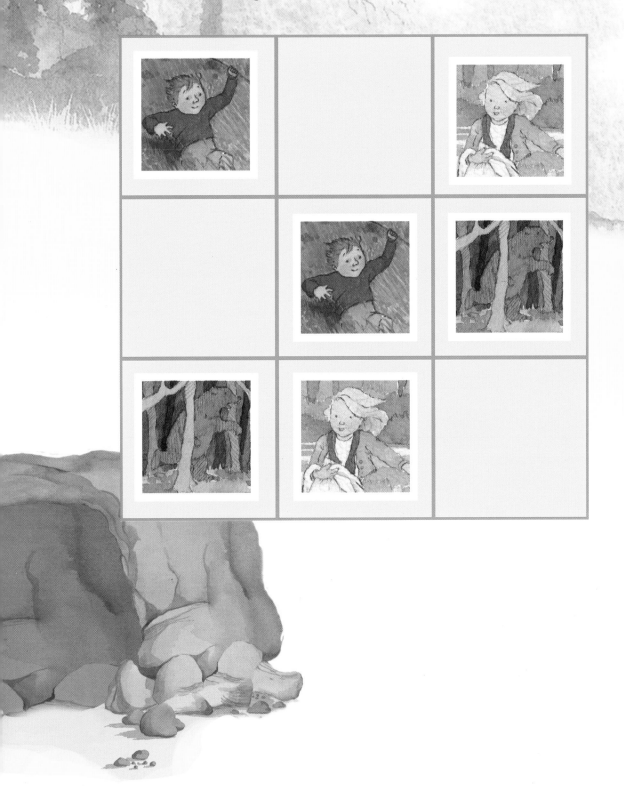

Do you know the bear hunt story?

Use your stickers to complete the adventure!

We're going on a ⬛ hunt!

First we swish swash through long wavy ⬛.

Then we find a deep cold ⬛ to splash splosh through.

Next we squelch squerch through thick oozy ⬛.

Uh uh! There's a big dark ⬛. We stumble trip through it.

On the other side there's a swirling whirling ⬛.

Finally we find a narrow gloomy ⬛ to tiptoe through.

What's that? It's a ⬛!

Run back home! We open our ⬛, rush up the stairs,

and jump into ⬛. We're not going on a bear hunt again.

What else could you go hunting for?

Perhaps a dinosaur, your favourite animal or even a monster!

Has it got big eyes? Does it have a tail?

Are its teeth sharp?

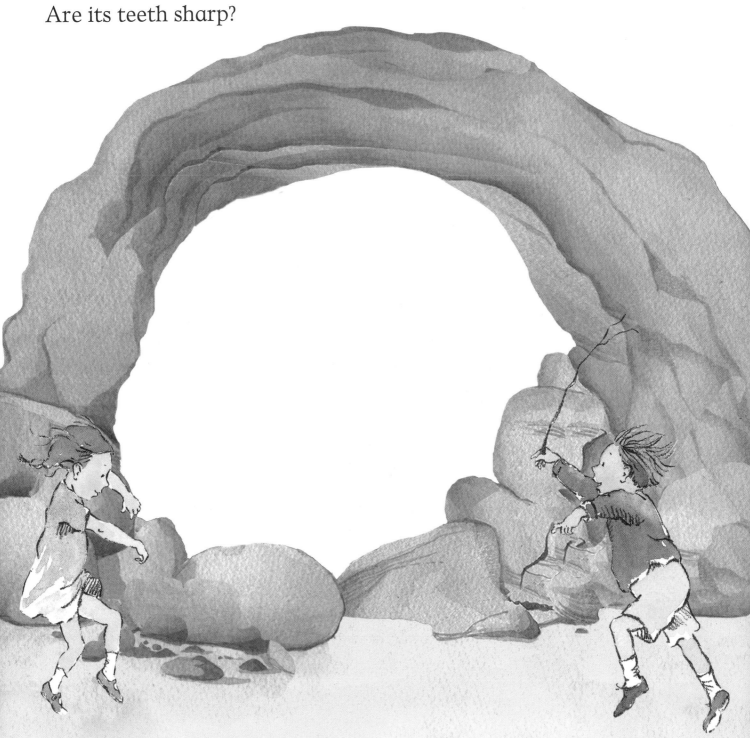

Finish the picture with some seagull stickers!

Spot the difference

There are six differences between the two pictures.
Can you find them all? Draw a circle
around each one.

Picture search

Can you find all the items below in the picture?

Circle each item as you spot it.

flying seagull

old tyre

dog

bird

standing seagull

bear

Odd dog out

Every dog below has a twin, except one. Match them up, then circle the odd one out.

What a tangle!

Follow the arrows to find out who is going walking with who, then draw a straight line connecting them.

Picture crossword

Use the clues below to solve this puzzle of the
bear hunt journey!

1. A big dark…

2. A swirling whirling…

3. Thick oozy…

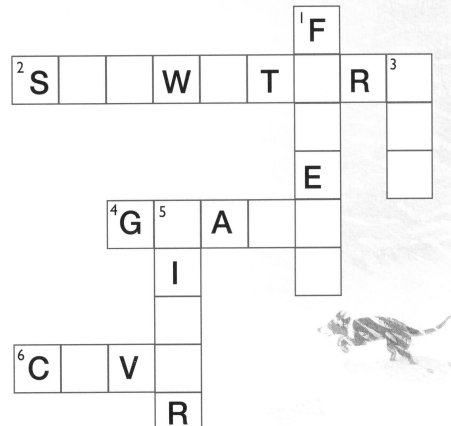

4. Long wavy…

5. A deep cold…

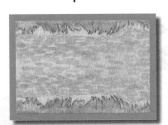

6. A narrow gloomy…

Find the bears!

There are nine bears hiding in this picture.
Can you find them all?

Sticker jigsaw

Use your stickers to finish the picture.

Join the dots

Connect the dots to finish drawing the boy, then use colouring pencils to draw in a background.

It's a mystery!

What do you think the girl could be pointing at?

Use colouring pencils to draw in your answer!

Nifty noises

Answer the questions below using your stickers.

What do you hear
in the grass?

What do you hear
in the forest?

What do you hear
in the river?

What do you hear
in a snowstorm?

What do you hear
in the mud?

What sound does
a bear make?

Where is the bear?

Draw the background, or make a collage
by sticking in pictures from old magazines.

Splash splosh!
Colour in the family to complete the picture.

Play the bear hunt game!

Stop to make a sandcastle! Go back one space.

Get blown away! Go ahead two spaces.

Follow a path throug the forest! Go ahead one space.

Slide through the mud! Go ahead two spaces.

Wellies full of water! Go back two spaces.

START

Get caught in a tide! Miss a turn.

It's a BEAR!

Trip over a branch! Go back one space.

How to play:

You will need one dice and a counter for each player – you could use different coins.

Start with the counters on the first blue space. Take turns to roll the dice and move your counter across the pages, following the instructions if you land on a yellow or purple space.

The first person to reach the cave is the winner!

Answers

Pages 2/3

Page 4

Page 7

Pages 8/9

Pages 10/11

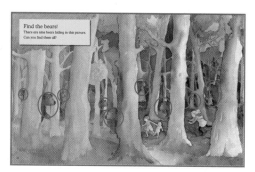

Pages 12/13

Page 14

Page 18

First published 2015 by Walker Books Ltd
87 Vauxhall Walk, London SE11 5HJ
10 9 8 7 6 5 4
Based on the bestselling picture book *We're Going on a Bear Hunt*
Original text © 1989 Michael Rosen
Text © 2015 Walker Books Ltd
Illustrations © 1989 Helen Oxenbury
This book has been typeset in Veronan Light Educational
The author and illustrator have asserted their moral rights
Printed in China
British Library Cataloguing in Publication Data:
A catalogue record for this book is available from the British Library
ISBN 978-1-4063-6192-6
www.jointhebearhunt.com
www.walker.co.uk

Page 3

Page 4

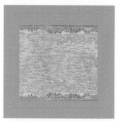 

Page 14

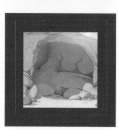 

Page 18

Hoooo wooooo

Growl!

Splash splosh

Stumble trip

Squelch squerch

Swishy swashy